By P.J. Shaw   Illustrated by Tom Brannon

Published by Creative Edge, 2010, an imprint of Dalmatian Publishing Group, LLC, Franklin, Tennessee 37067. No part of this book may be reproduced or copied in any form without written permission from the copyright owner. 1-866-815-8696

CE12680

Printed in the U.S.A.

10 11 12 NGS 10 9 8 7 6 5 4 2

"We're making *mail*," Zoe told Elmo and Abby Cadabby at the park one day.

"Cool!" Elmo said. "What kind of mail?"

"I am drawing a birthday card for *mí abuela*, my grandmother in Mexico," said Rosita.

"And I'm making a thank-you note for my ballet teacher," added Zoe.

"Ooh . . . those are so magical!" exclaimed Abby. "I've never had my very own letter before! Do fairies-in-training get mail?"

"I'm not sure," said Zoe. "But we have crayons and glittery stickers and markers. Want to make one?"

"Thanks, but I have to poof myself home now," said Abby. "My mommy says we're visiting Red Riding Hood's grandmother—or maybe it's the wolf. I can't remember."

"Abby has never ever gotten a letter before," Elmo told his goldfish, Dorothy, that night. "And Abby would like to have a letter of her very own. Wait a minute! Elmo can make a letter for Abby!"

So Elmo found some paper and crayons and asked his mommy for help. Mommy wrote two words at the top:

DEAR ABBY

"What comes next?" Elmo wondered.
"Something from your heart," said Mommy, giving him
a hug. "What do you think would make Abby happy?"

The next day after school, Elmo asked his friends for help.
"What was in Zoe's thank-you note?" Elmo asked Zoe.
"A picture of the Sugar Plum Fairy!" she answered.
"We're learning *The Nutcracker* ballet."

DEAR ABBY,

"Can Zoe draw the Sugar Plum Fairy for Abby?"

"Okay!" Zoe said, twirling on her toes. "Abby will love the Sugar Plum Fairy. She wears a fluffy pink tutu and a sparkly tiara!"

"If it's fluffy and sparkly you want, how about a picture of Little Murray Sparkles?" suggested Telly. "She's perfect for a fairy like Abby!"

"Thank you, Telly," said Elmo. "Would Baby Bear like to draw something on Abby's letter, too?"

Boing
Boing

"Hmmm . . . I shall draw Cinderella's enchanted carriage," declared Baby Bear, "because Cinderella's fairy godmother created it with a magic spell."

"Good idea!" said Telly. "And how about Cinderella on a pogo stick?"

"Pogo stick?!" asked Elmo.

"Sure," Telly said. "Who wants a carriage when you can *boing* your way to the ball?"

Later that day, Elmo carried Abby's letter to Nani Bird's tree.

"Oh, hello, Elmo," said Big Bird. "We're practicing our hopping. Now remember, Birdketeers, if you want to get better at something, it's important to practice. Keep hopping! I'll just stand over here and be quiet. You won't hear a tweet out of me!"

"Elmo is making a letter for Abby," Elmo explained. "Would Big Bird like to write something?"

"Sure, Elmo. Come on, everybody," Big Bird called. "Let's help write a letter to Abby!"

The Birdketeers drew pictures of daisies, stars, and butterflies—things a fairy might like. And Big Bird wrote a big **A** and **C**.

"**A** is for *Abby* and **C** is for *Cadabby*," he said proudly.

On his way to Bert and Ernie's, Elmo passed Oscar's trash can.
"Can Oscar help make a letter for Abby?" Elmo asked.

"I can, but I won't!" Oscar scowled. "Wait a minute. Maybe if I do,
little Miss Fairy Dust might wave that training wand of hers and fix
my Sloppy Jalopy. Here, gimmee that paper, fur face. Let's see now,
Abby likes pumpkins, right?"

"Ooh, Abby loves pumpkins!" Elmo said.

"Well, this one's nice and *rotten*," Oscar chuckled. "Now scram! I gotta give Slimey his mud bath. And, hey, don't tell anybody I drew that!"

"Okay, Oscar," giggled Elmo. "Have a rotten day!"

"Yeah, yeah," Oscar muttered. "Maybe it'll rain."

"Did I hear someone say *rain*?" asked Super Grover. "That is not good for swirly, adorable superhero capes!"

"Could Super Grover help make a letter for Abby?" Elmo asked.

"A letter? A *letter*? How about the letter **G**?" said Super Grover excitedly. "It has been very useful for this superhero."

And Super Grover scribbled a big, red letter **G**.

"Now, if you will excuse me, I have super-hero deeds to perform and monsters to save," he proclaimed. "Clear the runway! Up, up, and away!"

"Thank you," yelled Elmo. "Super Grover was *super* helpful!"

At 123 Sesame Street, the Twiddlebugs were having
a picnic in Bert and Ernie's windowbox.
"Elmo is making a letter for Abby," Elmo said.
"Would Bert and Ernie like to add something?"

"Gee, that sounds like fun, doesn't it, Bert?" asked Ernie. "Let's see, I'll draw a picture of Rubber Duckie and me playing hide and squeak."

"And I'll write down my favorite bird joke," said Bert. "That'll make Abby laugh!"

What's a pigeon's favorite holiday?
Feathers' Day!

When Elmo got to Prairie Dawn's house, everyone was practicing a play for Try-A-New-Food Day.

"Take it from the top!" Prairie shouted. "Oh, Elmo! We really need you to be a mango!"

"Elmo can be a mango tomorrow," Elmo said. "But Elmo is making a letter for Abby today."

"Oh, wait, wait! Me know something to put in letter!" Cookie Monster exclaimed. "It big and round and brown, and it start with letter **C**!"

"Cookie Monster," Prairie sighed. "Everybody *knows* it will be a picture of a cookie!"

"That what you think," said Cookie, drawing . . . a cantaloupe!

"It brown on outside and orange on inside," explained Cookie Monster. "Tasty anytime treat!"

Elmo thought and thought as he walked home on Sesame Street. What could Elmo put in Abby's letter? Abby liked rhyming words— words that sounded the same, like *house* and *mouse* or *play* and *day*. She liked Mother Goose and the Storybook School. . . .

"Greetings!" said Count von Count, appearing suddenly.

"Mr. Count? Elmo has a question," Elmo said. "Elmo wants to put something in a letter to Abby, but how does Elmo pick just one thing?"

"Why would you want to pick just one thing?" asked the Count.
"Choose two things, three things, ten things—twenty wonderful things!
Ah ah ah! Just think of all the possibilities!"

That night, Elmo made up his mind. He drew a special picture on
Abby's letter.

Then his daddy helped Elmo write a word at the bottom of the page.
Finally Elmo printed his name, nice and s-l-o-w.

And the next day, Abby got her very first letter. She was happy to see all the words and pictures from her friends on Sesame Street. And at the bottom of the page, she read . . .

DEAR ABBY,

A C

G

What is a pigeon's favorite holiday? Feathers' Day